D0612120

Cultivar

Adventures in the Liaden Universe® Number 25

Sharon Lee and Steve Miller

COPYRIGHT PAGE

CULTIVAR

Adventures in the Liaden Universe® Number 25

© Sharon Lee and Steve Miller, November 2017

Pinbeam Books

www.pinbeambooks.com

"Out of True" was first published on Baen.com, October 2013

"The Rifle's First Wife" was first published on Splinter Universe, January 2014

Both stories were collected in A Liaden Universe® Constellation Volume 3, Baen Books

August 2015

Cover design by Sharon Lee

ISBN: 978-0-9966346-6-3

NOTE

Cultivar is a horticultural term that refers to combining cuttings from the best plants to create a new plant with the finest characteristics.

A note on the existence of this echapbook. . .

Those who have been following the Liaden Universe® and/or the career of Sharon Lee and Steve Miller for a time will know that we'd gotten into the habit of producing chapbooks – 8.5x5.5 inch saddle-stitched pamphlets of 40-60 pages. The very first Lee-and-Miller chapbook was *The Naming of Kinzel*, collecting three fantasy stories featuring a well-meaning young wizard named Kinzel, which we published (it says here) in a limited run of 300, on June 20, 1987.

Later, SRM Publisher was formed, for the purpose of publishing chapbooks containing Lee-and-Miller, Miller, Lee, and, later still, other authors, work. This was in the age of paper; there were no ereaders, and computer screens were pretty rugged, still. For seventeen years, starting in1995, SRM Publisher produced at least one chapbook a year, at Yule, containing one or two Liaden stories.

SRM was closed in 2011, and we quickly realized that we weren't going to be able to break ourselves of writing short stories, so we established Splinter Universe (http://www.splinteruniverse.com[1]), where we would occasionally publish "splinters," i.e. pieces of stories or books that never came to completion, and also any new stories we happened to write.

Ever since SRM closed its doors, there had been a call from the readers who had been with the universe and the authors through all the changes, for the return of chapbooks. By now, technology had caught up with itself, so the authors began to produce echapbooks, on the model of the first paper chapbooks – and also republished all of SRMs backlist in ebook format.

---

1.   http://www.splinteruniverse.com/

At that point, the traditional publisher of our novels, Baen Books, suggested that they collect our stories into what was at first to be one volume. We agreed, realized that one volume wasn't going to be enough – so eventually *A Liaden Universe® Constellation Volumes 1* and *2* were published from Baen.

And that, should have been that.

Except – no, we *still* couldn't break ourselves of the short story habit, and the *Constellations* had done well for Baen. As soon as we had published enough short stories to warrant a book, Baen offered a contract for *A Liaden Universe® Constellation Volume 3*, which took several stories straight off of Splinter Universe. Those stories were never collected into chapbooks.

We recently realized that this was the case, and, in the interests of completeness, we have produced two echapbooks, collecting the four stories that were missed.

This is the first of those two "catch up" echapbooks, containing short story "Out of True," and novelette "The Rifle's First Wife."

This is what we said about each of those stories, in *Constellation 3*:

Out of True

One of the joys of working with a Baen books is their website, Baen.com, where Baen periodically releases stories free for reading to help celebrate upcoming book releases. We've been lucky enough to be asked to contribute on several occasions and when **Trade Secret** *was finally settled into a publication slot, Baen editor Tony Daniel asked for a* **Trade Secret** *related story. The problem was that the story needed to 1) have some obvious relationship to the novel, 2) not give away any major plot points of the novel or spoil future novels, and 3) be readable by new readers as well as long time Liaden fans. A close look gave us hope –* **Trade Secret** *had threatened to run away from us since there* *were places where more story could have been worked in. And, as it happened, we had some universe back-story that readers had been asking about for years. Combining the existing hook to the long-term requests got us to "Out Of True," a rather more serious story than we'd first expected.*

The Rifle's First Wife

Courtesy of a young man we didn't expect to survive his first meeting with Clan Korval, we get to look at the interplay of the suddenly mixed cultures of Surebleak. Needing to meet his new troop's expectations, Diglon Rifle, former enemy combatant, has been studying to become a more independent person. Noticed by Lady Anthora, he gets to work with plants, and to pursue his own individual interests – one of which happens to be card playing. What could go wrong? We had to ask this question because Diglon Rifle, much like the Taxi Driver and the Uncle, became far more of a character in the Liaden story than first expected. Enjoy – we did!

If this is your first time reading these stories, we do hope you enjoy them. And, for those of you re-reading, we hope you enjoy spending additional time with old friends found again.

—Sharon Lee and Steve Miller
Cat Farm and Confusion Factory
November 2017

Out of True

Squithen was gone from the forest clearing, which was good. The stench of the recent carnage was starting to reach him now and had it reached her she'd been here still, covering her nose as well as her eyes, counting or vocabing, one or the other.

Klay'd had to yell at her, which he never did, since she was so often cowed into incoherence by even a stern word, but then she'd heard him, flawlessly pilot-signed assent, and dashed like a smart-one into the bush, back the trail they'd followed here from the *Dulcimer*. Likely she'd really do everything he'd told her.

"Squithy, go to the cousins and tell them to bring big guns and hurry, because there *are so* monsters here like Choody said, and I killed one and maybe another. You run and be safe and stay there! Tell them we didn't find the uncles, but I'm trapped. Go!"

The dead things lay there across the small clearing, two or three of the tiny forms sundered into iron-blooded mess, another half-dozen more just laying there still, with shapes that looked broken and wrong even though he'd never seen any of them before, and the wicket monster mostly between him and the dead, holes in it's hide leaking dull copper. He could see heat or gas evaporating out of the husk, and dark splinters of structural bone where his third shot had struck home, right at eye edge of the thing.

It must have been that head shot, trying to hit *something* important, that had worked, stopping it long enough for them to flee and, in the end, dropping it in a heap. Good thing he'd had his training.

He'd been at the armorer's on Flason not too long ago, taking certification so he could carry on station, his pocket piece rousing extra interest from the staff there because of size of the pellet—it limited the carrying capacity yes, but it had stopping power. It had been his

5

great aunt's and come to him as the first of his mother's children to go off ship for a crew exchange. He was a decent shot on the targets and for three days he could see "Klay Patel Smith" at the top of the week's hottest shooter list at the shop. They'd called him Kid Klay, and that was fine–both the Patels and the Smiths were skinny as a rule anyhow and if they thought him young it made him feel better than being called undergrown.

So he was alive, at least, since they'd walked into the star-lit clearing and then that thing had charged straight on, discovered in the middle of crushing the small creatures–and he'd fired before turning and running, properly getting between Squithy and the trouble.

What he should have done was charge directly back the path they'd come in on, like Squithy did. Instead, he'd been doing an intercept course, like the compcourses showed. . .

The damnedest thing is that he was trapped, just like a couple of the small ones had been on the other side of the clearing. He'd run through a small bush and next thing he'd known was the scrape of branches and the rattle of leaves. The sound had confused him, and made him pause long enough that the web came down directly on him.

He was good and trapped and he might also be injured, his foot tangled in a knotted cord of fiber changing hue from green to blue and back again as he tried to search out a weak point. He was young–maybe the pain he felt was the twisted restraint and not a sign of actual damage. . .

He fretted, pinned under the heavy webbing, his good cutting and hacking tools all "safe and under eye" as the cousins wanted it, back at the ship, and Squithy not allowed to carry something with a sharp point or a good edge, on account of her being her, so she'd be best at the ship even if he was stuck. Didn't need an uncle to tell him to send the silly kid home and hope she survived and so could they.

The web was sticky around the edges, and multi-layered. Unlike the dead thing, the web was near odorless. One gloppy strand was slowly moving down the side of his face–not moving alive, but moving as the sticky stuff stretched away from his skin as he twisted slow. He tried that with his foot, and found some give there. Maybe now. . .he gave a great kick, like he was kicking open a recalcitrant locker door. . .

The pain was exquisite, wrapping his foot and leg with pressure and twisting it more.

His vision phased to full sight–he hadn't realized that he'd lost clear sight for a moment until it came back.

He thought back over what he'd seen, felt the stickiness on his face going softer again...

There it was–even his foot didn't feel as bad. So rapid twisting and pushing made the trap tighter. Slow effort–very slow–might work.

No way to be sure how long this had all taken, no way to be sure he'd ever see a one of help, given the cousins sitting there with the uncles out of the ship.

Squithy was the key. She was real sharp with a lot of stuff, but couldn't always reach it. She remembered patterns and numbers something fierce but she was scared of words. With Tranh and Rusko overdue, she was his hope, or he was.

He felt the breeze stir now, thought he heard one of those flying things in the distance. Maybe he heard something closer, but maybe it was the stuff on his face, drying in the breeze. Whatever made the noises, the wind brought with it more of the stink.

He felt his hand, the one still holding the gun. He could move it, and so he could shoot if he needed to, within much of his field of vision. Otherwise. . .if something came up behind him, say, he'd be in trouble.

Figuring that getting the stuff off from top down was the key, he moved as fast as he could, slowly.

It was hard to solve a puzzle from the inside, with both hands and both legs tied by gooey rope, and one hand needing to keep hold of the gun, just in case. It was harder with the breeze rising to colder and the star's illumination falling as it moved behind several of the overhanging trees. It did seem that as time went on the web-stuff was greener than blue, and that he could move faster. Maybe it was drying, or aging, or–

For a rare moment he wished that he was Squithy. Well, not that he *was* Squithy, but that he could have her absolute pattern recognition. He was sure that things had changed slightly in front of him, that the number of creatures appearing severely broken had fallen and that there were changes in the–

Yes, there were changes. Surely there's been six of the creatures hanging, apparently lifeless, in the web well across the way, and now there were three. Of the others–one of the remaining was no longer foot-caught, and there, had something in it's paw–in it's hand!–that was moving slowly.

"Murble la. Vemarmurble."

He'd been hearing little noises, like leaves moving quiet, to his right, where branches of the skinny trees tangled in high bushes. He couldn't turn his head quite that far to see what was happening, and he afraid to twist his whole body. Now, the sound grew to unknowable murmurs, like someone was talking real soft and long way away, talking in a language he didn't know. He listened, wondering if it was just those birds coming back. Birds made noises, flying things did, and some of them ate berries.

Still, with caution, he got his elbow a little looser from the gunky rope and raised it, to bring the aim of the gun lower. He'd had to shoot up at the creature who'd charged, but these sounds were lower to the ground, stealthy. . .

He heard now a distinct droning hum, and it came from across the clearing and from behind, it came from both sides and maybe even from the trees themselves. The sound rose, making it hard to keep track of the noises to his right, and then rose again as across the way brown, gray, and black furred creatures stretched, rolled over, sat up, stood up, turned to look at him, all at once, all unblinking.

Not all of the furry creatures were moving–but far more than he'd expected. Had they been stunned with fear? Paralyzed by the webbing? Yet the synchronicity of their movement was unnerving. And then the live creatures all blinked and stared at him at once and a kind of over-vision hit, as if he were watching a viewscreen through another viewscreen. More than that, he knew the drone was more than mere noise now.

He felt the questions more than heard them–not as if he was asked out loud in a proper language but buried in the drone–the idea, bouncing in his head until he knew that these weren't questions so much as demands: *Who do you know*, one was, accompanied by out of true images of a dozen or two humans, and the other was an image of Squithy–clear as a viewscreen straight on–with overtones of *where is* and *will she return?*

Klay had no answers and a lot of questions himself.

Klay was sure his voice was lost in the vast clearing; the trees had leaves that absorbed sound, the grass and bushes must surely do the same, the breeze itself–and the sound the creatures made.

"My name is Klay, and I'm stuck. Can you help me? Can you hear me?"

The ambient sounds quieted—he hadn't realized the creatures were making so many sounds as they moved, as stealthy as they'd been. Eyes were on him again, and this time when he heard the murbles he was sure there was variation in them. Across the clearing a small group of the furries gathered, motioning and mumbling together so there was not doubt that they were communicating something to each other—the question was, what? Surely they'd seen him shoot the creature—were they more afraid of *him* than they were of the dead things?

"My name is Klay Patel Smith and I need help. I've killed the monster. Can you get me out?"

Across the way now there were two of the creatures still hung up in the web-work, and only one of them active—and that one ignored now by the others, who were again staring in his direction, and as he managed to pull his left elbow free they gathered energy, moving in his direction.

Klay took a deep breath, carefully glancing to his elbow and using steady pressure peeled another inch or two of uniform away from the stringy mess, away from—

"Sssssss! Ssssss!"

He froze, hearing now not only another threatening sibilance but the giveaway sounds of movement close behind him. A tall green frond tipped with red fuzz swayed maddeningly on the edge of his sight, each movement accompanied by the sound of plant rubbing against plant.

The movement slowed, and then more of them bending and waving, until one frond end, much thicker than the rest, began to slowly lever downward into his sight, the swish of moving leaves accompanied by the low hum he was starting to recognize as the willful mumbles of the creatures he shared the battlefield with. Another sound got louder, but it was more than that, it was a vibration of the netting he was swaddled in. A moment of dislocation as he felt a fleeting touch of that mind-vision and now, perhaps the out-of-sight sound and vibration started to make sense as chewing or clawing.

Clawing?

Twung!

They were there, and they weren't attacking him. Instead, they were trying to help.

"Thank you," he called out, but the mumbles got loud.

He shivered, and only part of it was the result of major web-thread shaking and then going limp. Now the mumbles were murbles again, and that mind-vision was trying to get him to do what? He was getting a strange array of images, half of him and half like some fuzzy wraith in motion, like they wanted him to roll up into a ball!

Below him now, he saw heads and fists full of cord-wrapped stones. If he could pull his feet up some, tight, yes into a ball, the creatures could worry the rooted web easier.

The ball idea bounced around his head, and he risked trying to raise his feet, actually holding onto rather than denying the strands that held him. The web deformed around him, and another, much lighter twungging noise was greeted with acclamation from a multi-hued crowd that had grown from two or three to perhaps a dozen. The vibrations had grown to a constant, and he was bouncing as the creatures added their weight to his, stretching the overhead web at the same time they were tearing at the base.

His left boot and leg came away from the sticky base and he dared to grab a spot behind his knee with his hand. The bouncing increased and then his other leg was free.

That leg wasn't easy to pull up–Klay looked down and saw a face staring into his, a non-human face, somehow full of worry and concern and intent. The fur had silver-tips around the eyes and into the skull-top, with a dark almost black stripe swirling into brown around it.

The creature was testing his boot, he saw, gingerly touching his pants where they overlapped his boot, and. . .

He felt the concern enter his mind in the picture of something he didn't know–maybe a fruit. The picture of a fruit, sloughing its skin, and overlaying it the image of a foot–not his–falling away from a furred body.

Ah–he saw it, they were afraid they'd hurt him.

He looked at his left leg where he'd grabbed it, pulled on it to show that there was slack in the pants, thought at the creature of his leg inside the pants. . .

And the creature climbed then, grabbing his boots and then his pants, a free hand or paw wrapping a string of greenish vine around the webbing, stretching it to insulate or isolate the webbing from him, using a rock on a stick as a lever to pull the web away. . .

A loud murmur then, and a vision of Squithy running with others. At the same time an insistent vision of a fruit being pulled in many directions at once and the creatures around, including the one on his leg, all grabbing at web-strands and huffing and dashing straight away form him with their particular strands of the net. . .

Unexpectedly all the strands holding him parted, and he fell with bone jarring impact on his hip, the added weight of the silver-furred one twisting again that foot that had been sorely stressed to begin with.

"Dammit!" he yelled, and fought for breath. A flash of light tore through half-closed eyes, and a horrendous explosive thunder shattered the near-evening glade's urgent murbles into silence, leaving Klay's ear's ringing in the aftermath.

A high human voice screamed "No, no, no!" as he scrambled to get up and instead fell heavily, face down into a crowd of furry shapes.

The unfamiliar smell of dirt and vegetation assaulted his nostrils but he spent only a moment righting himself and lunging to his feet from an awkward crouch. Across the way were crew members, and around him, thigh high and shorter, a dozen of the creatures who'd freed him. He stood on uncertain legs, startled to find he still held the gun in near nerveless fingers.

The noise was all over there, where a chemical cloud drifted away onto the looming dusk.

On the edge of the clearing Squithy stood, red-faced and yelling, purposefully standing between Cousins Susrim and Falmer waving her arms, not just standing there but actively disrupting any chance any of the three had to aim.

"You can't! You can't. They're good!"

Klay yelled too, instinctively moving between his silver-fringed helper and the weapons being leveled in his direction, too.

"Stop. I'm fine, don't shoot! They helped me!"

Instinctively Klay moved his hands repeatedly palm down, miming the *slow slow slow* one might use on moving stuff dockside, "Stand down, damn it, just stand down!" he said, trying to insist across the distance and not willing to trust his foot to move.

A sigh went through the glade, as if a wind of hums and murbles had worshiped itself into a breathy quiet, and all around, the creatures seated themselves where they were, silent and expectant, watching him, watching Squithy. Waiting.

Klay sat quiet in his berth, staring at familiar walls, waiting for a decision. The decision. What decision he wasn't sure of.

He'd studied some star charts. He'd thought of how it would be if he was in charge, what he'd change, what he'd keep the same.

Wasn't really wasn't up to him, but he thought hard about it, writing a file in his head but not recording it anywhere. Rusko and Trahn Smith—his uncles, officially—were Senior Pilot and Captain, and they were Trader and Senior Trader, one by one. For that matter they were Senior and standard everything else on the ship, from 'ponocists and medicos to tech and cooks and the cousins—Cousins Susrim and Cousin Falmer and Cousin Squithy—they were all general crew, 'cept they should have been more, but maybe not Squithy.

Anyhow, *usually* not Squithy.

And since he was a pilot and a tech, and mobile, too, at the moment he was back-up everywhere, a hardly known outside cousin to the general crew who'd lived the ship since birth. All awkward, and needing a cure.

Their ages, that was the problem, their ages and their experience. Everyone but Trahn was almost too young to be what they was, the ship having come to them after a really stupid firefight on Trask-Romo took out Trahn's Da and Ma, who were Squithy and Susrim and Falmer's parents too.

Susrim was studied to be cook and arms, and was up to a local back-up pilot rating any day now, but he didn't have the credits from a recognized school or committee yet. Falmer, she was one cycle behind Susrim in age but ought to have been head cook awhile back, but Susrim was studied there and she wasn't. Falmer had some medico stuff and was in charge of Squithy when Trahn wasn't, which it turned out was most of the time. At the moment Trahn was Falmer's ward, hard as that was on both of them.

Captain Trahn was where he was because he took the warguilt payoff the bar came up with on account of the bloodshed and boom, brought in pretty Uncle Rusko, who'd not been much of a fit on *his* home ship despite his top grade piloting, on account of that ship, *Proud Plenty*, was looking for blood-heirs, and then that meant *Groton* needed a Patel or a Smith, and when it all filtered down through a standard of people-trades from ship to ship–Klay'd ended up here, on a ship where neither the Captain nor the Senior Pilot had ever run a crew meeting, and where the crew, aside from him and Rusko, had never even *been* in a real crew meeting on account of the *Dulcimer's* departed owners hadn't run a crew-share ship.

Now–well things had changed when he'd come out of hydropnics, where he was back-up to the injured Trahn. Trahn's legs. . .not good. One was broke just below the knee, and the other was ankle sprained. Falmer had seen one of those problems for real in life, meaning everything getting done doing was by the file and devices, not from experience.

Rusko had cornered Klay yesterday, he being the mobile one of the high command at the moment, a finger-to-lip followed by beckoning motion bringing them both outside to the rough camp still in place beside the ship. They stood well within the clearing, the usual camp followers lounging watchfully around the fringes of the three new paths they'd made for themselves, and sometimes watching the path to the fight-scene.

"I see seven of them," Klay'd offered, not trusting that there weren't two dozen more sitting behind the weeds laughing at them. It wasn't that they were malevolent–but that they were so quiet and sneaky when they weren't talking to themselves or each other.

"Quick eyes, Pilot," Rusko said then, "really quick eyes. Squithy tells me that there's seven of them here most times but not the same seven–that three of them hang out all the time together and–she says they are living here–but the others change off. She's being a regular field biologist!"

"But she's not here with them right now. . ."

Rusko smiled a wan smile–"No, I had to come get her and ask her to talk to the Captain. She hasn't had a word to say to him, seems like. We need to get some stuff cleared up real soon. . ."

He'd let that sentence go reluctantly, and took up again, with a sudden urgency.

"Normally, on most ships, this is something command ought to know but not official. But since this is all so odd, we need to get things clear. Can you tell me what you've done–I mean, are you and Squithy playing pair?"

Klay shook his head as the recalled, remembering that he'd burst out laughing and then shook his head at the time.

"Muddy tracks, have you lost your mind?"

Rusko'd sighed, and held his hands up.

"It doesn't matter to us, really–you're split cousins far enough away that's not a matter. But here, understand where we're coming from. And I mean *we* in this since it has been bothering Trahn so fierce."

Klay'd waited, maybe not patient, and Senior Pilot had made hand-talk of something like *clear glide path* before speaking again.

"Something happened. We know something happened. It wasn't just that you shot that thing, hard as that must have been, but did something happen between the pair of you before then? Because we all know that Squithy now isn't the Squithy she was before. And if she got that way because you paired in the bush that'll do for us. We just need to know. . ."

Klay knew it, he'd known it for sure the moment she'd stepped in front of the guns between her cousins and the clearing. She *was* changed—and he was afraid he knew why. He'd played it over a bunch of time in his head, wondering if the shock of the attack had done it, or if the air had done it.

"All we did was what I told the crew we'd do. Hadn't heard from you, so we walked out the trail you'd marked to the clearing, part-ly for some exercise, partly looking for you. Comms were coming up empty—not even time signal—and we figured, that is *I* figured three hours overdue was pushing things. It was on my head since you'd told Susrim and Falmer to stand tower watch.

"Got out the trail, and there you weren't. Hiked on to the clear-ing with three paths out, like you said, but the clearing wasn't emp-ty—there were all the creatures there, trying to get some of them out of the webs, the rest quiet and waiting and watching, and then Choody's monster came in and—"

"The fight stuff, we have that recorded Klay, what you told us, and what you told Susrim right then. There's a couple things we'll need to talk about there, but some of it I'll have to clear with Trahn anyhow before I can say a word on it."

Klay hand signaled *acknowledge.*

"I mean, it all happened so fast. The thing broke out of the woods of a sudden, and it was like it looked at the littles and was just going to eat them all—I mean, we knew that's what was going to happen, we could feel it!—and then it looked at us, and Squithy yelled, "No, you can't, Tobor! Klay, stop it!' and it looked at us and made that charge. . ."

He'd done the rehash twice more, from different directions, the while they walked the perimeter of the clearing. By the end of their walk one of the creatures, the one Klay called Oki, the one who'd done the most to free him, had come to them and walked as if part of the conversation for a turn, and then natural as could be grabbed Klay's hand and pulled himself on Klay's shoulder, the usual low murble of greeting suffused with the gentle mental touch he thought was a hello, or maybe a request for news or–something.

The expression on Rusko's face went from horrified to resigned with a shake of his head.

"Susrim told me that you and Squithy have both been too friend-ly with these things. I didn't believe you'd let them up in your face, though!"

Klay shrugged, the paw on his shoulder support enough for his rider.

Rusko stepped back with a sigh.

"I can't believe I need to ask you this, now. But I do. First, please put the creature down."

There followed a modest contest of will, and in fact the creature came down, leaning for a moment against Klay's leg until a strong glance and hand motion chased Oki away. The creature retreated a dozen or so steps and Klay looked meaningfully toward the nearest of the three paths, and waited until Oki started in that direction.

"He's down."

Rusko saluted the obvious and went on alert pilot status, pulling away his quiet and putting on the command aspect he seemed to shun when it came to people.

"Tell me this. This is professional evaluation, this is a command evaluation. Could you feel confident as a Pilot in Charge, assuming neither Trahn nor I was available? Could you take *Dulcimer* to the next port with current crew? Could you finish a cargo route with current crew sans Pilots One and Two?"

Klay'd blinked, thought to the boards, thought to the ship, thought to the crew.

"You're asking if I'd have taken–could have taken the ship on if we hadn't walked out from the clearing and found you? Or if you'd been killed instead of just have bruises and breaks?"

Rusko nodded, said, "Yes, exactly. If the cave in had killed us both, would you have been able to survive–either call in Choody or just get to the next port, which might have been better."

Klay harrumphed, sighed, nodded.

"Yes. The first–just to the next port–It wouldn't have been pretty, but it wouldn't have been hard, really, other than bodies or lack of 'em. The second thing–moving on–would be harder and we'd need some signature cards we don't have so I could sign for cargo and expenses–I hadn't got that far. But crew from number three down, yeah, we can run the ship. Shall I make a report for you?"

Rusko's turn to blink. Then: "You're positive?"

Klay's nod brought a quiet whistle from the pilot, who'd surveyed the ship and the landing zone solemnly, and echoed a nod.

"I'm going to be asking everybody the same question and so will Trahn. The ship's got to be sure of itself. Don't discuss this with anyone until were decide what we're going to do."

The stuff about Squithy. . .he thought on that some more. Hadn't much thought of her as a partner possible. Hadn't much thought about anyone being with Squithy. Wasn't impossible, but you like to feel the person you were talking to was on the same wavelength, and that didn't happen all that much with Squithy, in his experience. Or hadn't. But once they'd secured the clearing she'd been right there in helping find their way, and keeping the furries out of their way. More, she'd even told him she asked the creatures if they'd seen Tranh and Rusko, and they'd pointed the way. Then they'd walked them all the way back to the ship and circled 'round the clearing like they owned the place, trying to take Squithy to the three paths. She'd been patient with them, like she was paying attention and knew things that weren't just if her blood pressure was good or if she'd seen seventy-seven red things on the day.

So really, if he ran the ship he'd just put her on breakfast once a week, just to test her...

The rarely used PA system burped a scratchy high volume tone, bringing the startled Klay to his feet. Following the noise came the *pfffft* of some quick-huffing test of the microphone link, and then Rusko's quiet matter-of-fact voice.

"*Dulcimer* crew meeting for all hands begins in five minutes. Bring with you any local plants or wildlife in your possession, please. All crew members includes you, Squithy, no matter what you're doing. Five minutes, be prompt."

On the third day of Jump, Rusko on Board One and Klay on Two, Falmer was still sitting with Tranh. The break swelling wasn't going down so well for Tranh and he had some infection, so he'd been hit with heavy duty antibiotics and general relaxants to make him be quiet. He'd been able to hold the basic meeting before the lift, using the logbooks that Klay'd pointed out to him and some agenda templates Squithy'd dug out of ship-files. Basic meeting was a promise to make longterm changes–and a Captain's Apology for having screwed up a run.

"Choody got me to go where he wouldn't go, and now that I'm injured won't come through on the pay for us having been there. So this is a ship-rule: *Dulcimer* don't deal on bar-deals without crew input. That a rule. Also, *Dulcimer's* not dealing with Choody, nor coming back to Thakaran, as long as I'm on the deciding side. That's a rule."

He paused then, having shifted slightly and then gone white trying to move his leg a little with his hand. I'll put you two"–that was said to Susrim and Falmer–"to finding long-range replacement runs for us to think on. Given Choody and his connections we're going to be dropping as many of the old runs as we can – Da never did make it big, and he kept rubbin' against the underside figuring he'd get a deal. But we're out of that side now–another ship's rule, no dark trading. I got some stuff Da and Jenfer left us, and. . .some other things. . .that we ought to be able to move quick as can and be good. Then straight cargoes, all."

At that he'd said, "That's after Port Chavvy," leaned back in his seat with half closed eyes, and said "Rusko's got the rest of it. It'll be a boring run out cause we're not for Choody's station, but we're set foodwise. Rusko's on after me."

At that he'd stared at Falmer and smiled. "Now I'll take that painloss you gave me, right?"

With that he pressed a patch against his wrist with a sigh, and waved his command hand one more time, wiping a little sweat off his forehead, and said "We're going to Port Chavvy because we still have a Founding Member share there, so we can port as long as we need to while we spook up more business. You guys got work to do!"

Rusko'd done well, all things considered, and they'd planned their shifts as best they could, including Squithy in some, including the business of trying to shoo away the

norbears, which Susrim had named by accident.

"I tried looking those things up," she said, "and all I got is images and notes–and they never was mentioned to be here on Thakaran. Couple of entries that they've been seen with scouts. Warnings from a couple sectors that they're contraband. Standing offer from Crystal Biogenics, and a competing one from University. Biogenics is paying a haul of cash for a Standard's visit, and University's looking for a breeding pair but don't talk money–

"And more, couple smuggler's myths that they showed up around old tech sites on a couple planets, no sense why, but that's it. A dozen different names, calling them shore dogs and green apes and some Liaden stuff that translates into sleepy bear Terrans. But they're not. They're mammals, but they are not dogs nor green apes nor bears!"

She'd scrunched up her face when she'd said it, and Squithy had laughed out loud without it sounding like hysterics for once, and repeated the words, pushed together.

"Norbear. If they aren't dogs or cats or dragons they're norbears!"

Which had put a cap on the all together part of the discussion since Tranh had fallen asleep.

Klay was still sore from some bruises, but that was minor compared to Rusko's–he tended to complain about the stiffness in his arms, and Falmer's suggestion that pulling Tranh out of the fallen cave roof had strained him apparently annoyed the pilot to the point of snippiness.

Still, ship stuff was going on and it being just before shift change he wasn't surprised entirely to see lights showing movement. . .

"Where's Falmer?" he asked, watching the lights.

"You need analgesic? Falmer's sticking with Tranh."

"Isn't Squithy on breakfast?"

"She is–you can go first if you need. . ."

"So that means Tranh's in with Falmer, Squithy's doing breakfast, you're here, I'm here, and Susrim's on sleep."

He'd gotten Rusko's attention, saw raised eyebrow and quick glances to housekeeping boards.

" 'ponics door has opened a couple times here. . ."

Rusko made a noise that might have been a complaint, and reached to touch a tab.

"Susrim?"

Klay thought he'd heard motion over the connection, but the sound ceased.

"Pilot Rusko here, is that you, Squithy?"

A light noise then, and another, and—

"murble. . ."

Klay was out out of his seat instantly –

"We've a 'norbear" stowaway!"

"This isn't good! Take it," Rusko ordered. "And get Squithy to help you."

Klay ran, half-bouncing off the slide-door on his way out.

"I thought so!" was what Squithy said, her step light behind his as they squeezed into the right angle passage. There were marks in the passage, in fact all up and down the passage, some scuffed over, some clear, near handlike foot prints in white.

Klay looked toward the lower corner where the door would open first–but Squithy was moving in that direction.

His palm hit the waist-high release, wondering if the faint hand-shaped mark there was dangerous far too late, and the door slid open, Squithy on one knee, ready to catch. . .

Ready to catch the norbear, who, rather than rushing to escape was sitting quietly in a comfortable pose on top of Growcase C, star-ing at the greens, sipping from a wide-mouthed sampling bowl, a trail of splashes and white spots leading back to the push-spigot. Both arms were white, and there was a vague halo whitish about the chest.

"Oh, good!" said Squithy. "Holdhand herself!"

"Holdhand? You know this one?"

"'ponics? What's happening?"

"Murble lamurbla," said the norbear, using bright care to sit the cup down without spilling, it, and glancing at the speaker. Then, she reached toward Squithy, offering her hand to hold.

"Norbear is in here in 'ponics, Pilot. Admiring the carrots, I'd say."

"Capture it. We'll have to put it out an airlock I guess."

By then Squithy had the norbear in her arms, and stared up at the speaker, the murbles almost drowning out out her denial.

"You can't, Rusko. They saved Klay." Her voice quavered then and rose in volume to a whine dangerously like Squithy of old.

"Squithy, don't start now. We figure out a way to make it quick but..."

"Stop talking!"

That sounded even more like Squithy of old...

Klay ventured "Rusko, let's..."

Squithy held onto the creature, cuddling her...

"It's my fault she's here! She believed me when I told her we'd be leaving and never coming back to that planet. And now she's here. She's a widow and she came here because Klay's here to keep us safe and...Oh no!"

Klay say her stare behind him and turned as a chorus of murbles broke out behind him. He heard Squithy, but it didn't sink in immediately, she was going on and on about something–

"Rusko, Pilot! Don't you see, they think slow and it helps me thinks slow. And they saved Klay and they make me real crew! And it isn't all of them, just..."

Klay saw two more of the norbears at the door, these even more covered in white, the flour falling off of them and falling on to the floor and on the tiny creatures they held to breast and who clung to their feet, the trail of flour down the passage toward dry stores...

"The widows, Rusko, only the widows came."

Squithy looked hard at him, but he'd already noticed the shy touch of a hand at his knee, heard the murbles.

"We'll have to talk, Rusko," Klay said steadily. "We'll have to be convincing for Trahn!"

"What's Trahn got to do with it? This is on my. . ."

"That Crystal Biogenics, Rusko. I'm guessing they're about as dark as you can get and still be seen. But they'll probably take Trahn's old tech, and whatever you're hiding from that cave, too."

"Murble?"

"What?" The last speaker was Rusko, the former was the norbear climbing to be held, and the reaching for the beaker of water Holdhands had left on the greens case.

"I'm thinking we've got a little clean-up to do. . .might need some help. The widows and kits, they're a little dusty. Guess the place is a little out of true."

Port Chavvy was being a challenge for *Dulcimer*, both internally and externally. They'd been on port four days, and the problems. . .

Rusko'd been threatening calling sabotage and spacing the lot of the norbears, and Squithy and Klay with them. While he wasn't quite serious only the slowly improving health of Tranh cheered him at all—while he swore they'd not lift ship until the stupidity of several generations of Smiths and Patels was cured.

They'd rented a tool rack, which sat here externally—it had taken cash up front to get it delivered, and promise of a full-time responsible guard to let it stay. That stricture had Squithy get all antsy because she thought, it being "all her fault for thinking too fast and thinking too hard," she ought to be guarding it—which no one wanted beside her, since the norbears were all over her wherever she went. She could be gone a few minutes at a time, but after that, they got restless.

Internally, the rack meant Klay got elected for most guard time while Falmer, Susrim, and Rusko did clean up and Tranh fumed and took his meds, Falmer having convinced the port hospital that med-officer meant med-officer without having to transport Tranh the whole way down there.

Klay peered at the rack, as he was supposed to from time to time, counting the tools and checking the inventory sheet. Squithy'd been out just once, Falmer four times, and Rusko once. Rusko was currently making sure the free-stacked stuff from the cleaned hold was still under watch, and grabbing a couple of breaths of flourless air as well.

The flour–shouldn't have happened. The norbears had found the unsecure dry-food storage door and wandered in, Squithy's vague information about laying down for lift-off giving them an urgency which brought them to push things around so the kits could snuggle against their moms. Then some of the kits had discovered pulltabs, and gone on a binge of bag openings, and others of the kits. . .had found the secret door.

For like all indie spacers, the Smiths and the Patels fancied themselves could-be smugglers–just like Tranh and Rusko had with their secret deal to gather Old Tech for Choody!– and they'd their hidden compartments and secret latches and. . .and then the elders gunfought and lost without telling their ship kin the wheres and whens of things.

Klay'd yet to see all of it. He'd heard enough to see what had happened–the discovered cubby holes had led to a secret compartment with some secret stuff in it, and that fed to another place, and the kits having figured out latches had ended up in closet of the ship's full toolroom, and thus–once the air ways was open–the ship's automatics and stinks systems had started up with vengeance. The tools, the stores, several passageways, all covered in flour.

Rusko, a neat man at all times, only had a little flour on him.

"Everything's coming along," he said before signing out another hand-pull airspray, "and we got Trahn doing inventory inside. There's a lot of cleaning going on. . ."

Klay nodded, and asked, "How's she holding up?"

She, of course, was Squithy. She'd run herself ragged the day before, finally getting the norbears to understand how they could help–and what "stay out of the way" meant.

"I'm watching her, and I swear it feels like she's finally figured out how to pace herself. She's doing good."

"Do you believe her?"

Now that was a loaded question, since it brought in norbears, which they all agreed they wouldn't mention, not even to each other, outside the ship–and it also put Rusko on the spot. If he believed the whole thing–that Squithy hadn't let them into the ship on purpose, but had simply explained they were going away, and told them about the ship. . .and they'd got the details of how things worked by listening to her and watching her mental tour of the ship. . .and that they'd got the idea that having their families somewhere where there were no Tobors to trap and eat them was a good thing all on their own.

Rusko looked away, following the progress of an odd group of crewmen, all of an almost golden skin tone, all small–smaller than Klay, for sure, and a couple of them dressed like–like–rich folk.

"What are they, Liadens?"

Klay laughed.

"What else? They've been stomping up and down the dock every few hours–guess it must be exercise class. Got themselves a tradeship like hardly stops here. They asked me "what ship" the first three times I saw 'em, but they've stopped. We're boring."

Rusko snickered.

"Liadens! Space sure is getting strange, isn't it?" Rusko fiddled with his airspray, making it pfffufff a couple times.

"It is, isn't it?" Klay agreed. "And Squithy?"

Rusko shrugged.

"Well, asked that way, she's not as strange as she was. I'm thinking she's not out of true anymore, all told."

Klay fixed Rusko's eyes with a straight look, asked "And so that means. . ."

"That means we're not looking to offload her anytime soon, or you, or the. . .excess cargo. I'll send her out with a handwich. You'll be wanting to get used to having her around."

The Rifle's First Wife

The sweat felt good to the Rifle; the effort did, the whippy wind gusts and sudden lulls providing an extra challenge to a course laid out in part by the blind necessity of defunct mining machines and part by the will of men long gone. Clan Korval and their minions had yet to exercise their will on most of the land, other than bringing the impossible tree and likewise impossible house to what had been a quarry, and starting an experimental joint farm with the bordering landholder.

In the distance, seen between the spiky path-side thistle-grass, were rows of extra hardy vegetables – and many days he was among them, along with the small expert who was Alara chel'Voyon, Field Ecologist. Thus did Line yos'Phelium, Clan Korval, dispose of his time this work stretch, for which he was not at all unglad.

He held a look in that direction momentarily: sometimes she acknowledged his passing, as did all of the folk here, particularly those in charge. She'd been there today when he started his run, but Alara wasn't visible now, nor her field kit. He'd been concerned these last several days, that he'd not been performing his duties properly, or that the anomalous results they'd had were discovered to have been due to some error of his. The ecologist's usual low-key banter had been missing, and she both shorter of temper and of praise.

"Did you triple measure? Have we got the image?" Not only had she asked such self-evident questions, but at the end of the day yesterday she'd neither offered a Liaden bow or a Terran-style wave, merely pointing out that she'd see him on his next work shift in the fields.

In going over the social parts of his interactions with the biologist it seemed too that Alara—as she expected to be called for the everyday work transactions—had been less talkative for some few days, perhaps even from the last morning in the city. Something was perhaps not in order, then, at the center of her work. . .or in her need to come out to the fields, as much as she sometimes seemed to enjoy it. His duty, of course, was set by others.

He did not dispute Korval's right to place him in the fields with a sometimes sharp-tongued Scout who was bent on making each and every plant in the experimental rows grow larger and more edible than the one next to it. They owned his oath, did the yos'Pheliums, and if his fitness for work in the fields was determined by the one the Explorer called Scout, it was not his to deny it.

It had seemed odd at the first that he'd passed review with not only the elder Scout, who had taken their temp oath in order to see one of the Troop reach medical care while there was still hope, and then the Scout and the Captain, to whom Nelirikk was expressly sworn, but also had been presented to the Scout's almost respectably sized cousin-called brother, a sub-commander and his wife–Shan yos'Galan and Priscilla Mendoza–and then, to the machine that wandered the house feeding cats, and to the woman Anthora, also a yos' Galan.

That one, oh, that one. She'd looked to him at first like a cuddle-girl, impossibly tiny and soft, vulnerable and needing protection. . .and then she'd really looked at him. Her eyes–he still blinked at the thought of her eyes, never doubting that she was one of the Liaden witches he'd been warned of in training, and never doubting, either, the warmth of her smile as the several kittens had wrestled at his feet.

It was the kittens he thought, and the hearty Terran-style nod Lady Anthora gave, that had brought him to the work in the field: she'd turned to the Captain and the Scout and said, "This one will much prefer growing things to shooting things, once he is used to it."

And then she'd laughed, turned back, and told him to always mind the cats, if they spoke to him, and wandered off.

His breath was comfortably labored, and he turned for the last of the run, preparing, and then busying himself as he usually did with a sprint to finish.

The tree shadowed him now and in that shadow he felt an extra warmth, as if the tree's very bulk forced the winds to flee before its willingness to stand firm, or else that it exuded a welcome to those who belonged.

Belonging to a world was an unusual thing–he'd grown up as a man of arms, expecting that all he belonged to was the Fourteenth Conquest Corps. That was when The Yxtrang High Command had been his decision maker, a time he was, in retrospect, glad was over. He had stood on seventeen worlds in his life, counting this one, and this was perhaps the third where he stood somewhat welcome. Large by most Terran standards, to Liadens he was out of reason large, overly muscled, and menacing. He'd discussed Liad's reaction to him with the Explorer, Nelirikk, who also owed allegiance to Korval's uncanny leaders and their line, and the Explorer had it that Surebleak welcomed them, and that Liad must be considered a toss-up.

While breath being caught back to normal, he shook his hands, stretched his arms, allowed the thoughts he'd been thinking to creep back to the world, the people he knew here, and his duty to Line yos'Phelium. A spray of dust carried a flimsy light-green leaf, and he bowed to temptation, and swept it from the air, noting approximate time, and shoved it in his pocket. He'd recognize it, or the Field ecologist would. . .

As was, then, it was otherwise a wild and strange world, here, far from the spaceport he was posted to as a shift guard every other ten day, and the weather, though seasonally warm by local standards, was uncertain as it always was, and then bordering frigid. He'd fought in more comfortable places.

And then he was back in a calm provided by the towering tree overhead and the outer walls of the tiny fort-like house that enclosed its base. He had not worn off the euphoria of run, and that was good.

His run had been a moderate one, by choice, given his evening plans, and he'd received the news that he'd exceeded his average time for the relumma by a healthy four percent. The rest was due, he expected, to his concentration on thoughts other than running, and to the fact that one of his objects of consideration had been visible during his courses.

"Hello, I am present in the house," he said, having entered the small side-hall that he and other staffers used, "and on rest day. Is there need for me to alter my schedule?"

The "house" in term of personnel was not only the security 'bot, but also a butler, several house folk, a cook, a handyman, and himself and sometimes his several non-clan superiors. Elsewise, guesting in the house could be just about anyone, ranging from Boss Conrad, ruler of the world, to children of Korval clan members, to cats, to visiting scouts, pilots, musicians, and just strange odd folks. Since he was on garden security at this time rather than house security, his position didn't require him to report to the butler as long as the 'bot knew of him. . .not that reporting to the butler was onerous, though one did sometimes have to search the maze of rooms for some time to find him.

This was day six of this tour of what he called Tree Home; day six was a day largely of his own necessities, a luxury he appreciated very much. That his immediate superior was on duty elsewhere this day made it even less likely than normal that he would be interrupted at his private studies and work. That he was permitted private study and work–was far beyond luxury. That he, Diglon Rifle, the only certified Rifle on this world–even the only one in this system!– would have R&R leave this evening would have astonished someone more used to allowing such concepts their sway.

He had always been a simple man. Through creche and schooling and training, and through seven rotations of the vaunted Fourteenth Conquest Corps, he'd taken what life brought with little question, accepting the rights of others to order his presence and actions: it was a given that a soldier of the Yxtrang would revere honor and order, and even orders themselves, requesting little for himself. It was only lately that his life had taken an odd turn for an Yxtrang, for now he was oft expected to both know and to pursue his choices when they did not conflict with the needs of his superiors.

He had spoken on entry, knowing that the house, in the person of the security bot Jeeves, was already well aware of his presence, if not by the touch of his hand to pressure plate, then by the weight of his step on the foot mat at the door, or the sound of his breathing. It was the way things were properly done, the announcement, and few on the planet Surebleak was as happy to do things the way they were done, as was he.

The house had delighted by giving his run time and allowing to know that no schedule change was required.

"Welcome, Diglon Rifle. The research information you requested is available; shall I save files to your data trees, deliver hard copy to your quarters, or deliver by voice as you work? Shall I mark this restricted personal, general research, or place it in the open query bin?"

It bothered him that he was addressed in Yxtrang troop mode, but it was part of his duty to the new Captain he was sworn to. Perhaps he should ask if he might be free of that on his day off. . .

The voice had been practicing with someone, or several some-ones; not only was the inflection closer than it originally had been to that of active troopers, now it began to come close to the proper ac-cent and timing as well. True, the voice had also been practicing with *him* but he felt that the inflections were likely due to study and di-alogs with his elders-in-former-troop.

Diglon had long ago gotten over the odd fact of the robot's ap-parent self-animation and personality as well as his seamless inte-gration into house systems; in fact he'd long ago gotten over many things about his new station in life. That was a troop's job after all: to put behind past actions and necessities in order to concentrate on the present order set, to follow orders, to. . .

Well, he thought, a rare Terran sound momentarily burying a phrase translated out of Liaden for a phrase out of Trade, and then the stutter as the Terran, direct from the Captain, returned to echo across his life, having lost the war to irony and become fact.

The Yxtrang concept, learned at first by a story told by an elder Troop, was rote as a child and reinforced at first once per ten day and then once per five day and then once per day until at last it was part of his very waking thought: *Today I will joyfully do the work of the Troop, without delay, remorse, reserve, or restriction.*

That the head of local security was both a bot and available to him as an unparalleled library of information resources. . .well then, he understood that the bot had once been a butler for Clan Korval and a war robot. The robot, then, was of the troop as much as he. . .

"Please, place it in my day file, under personal," he said, elated, moving through the halls leading to what once had been servants quarters and now was security's small corner of this house under tree. He could use a shower, and then study. On impulse, he added "On my non-duty day I would prefer to speak in one of the locally used languages, if that is practical."

"As you say, Rifle." Those tones were in a strict Terran, without recourse to the Surebleak slang the troop was also absorbing.

The idea that he might have an access-restricted personal file that his troop mates and even his immediate superior might not enter at whim–an amazing thought that had frozen him for minutes the first time it was explained to him–continued to elevate him. That he could alter policy by expressing his wish! The Conquest Corps had been inadequate!

"This troop, this Line yos'Phelium, Clan Korval," Nelerikk Explorer had explained early in his relationship with the house, "is a troop of victors. It functions well by following orders and commands, as any well-organized troop may be expected to function, but it is victorious because it assumes and it demands that all troops are capable of making decisions. Personal initiative is not only expected, it is required. From the very oldest to the very youngest, all are expected to exceed norms, to excel at their own assigned duties as well as at duties or arts they choose themselves. Culture, arts, science, skills of joy or skills of survival, it is not expected that any one owing allegiance here should be backward in the pursuit of accomplishment. One must study what is at hand, and seek to improve the lives of all."

His independent accomplishments thus far included a modest facility with the Trade language and likewise a modest facility with Terran, many words of Liaden if not a fluent speaking ability and a well-studied ongoing interest in the casual games of chance he was able to take part in when on Portside duty, where games of cards were a staple of the day's schedule. There his tendency to taciturn study of

his hand did him well, and had led to his part in a public card tour-
nament, and then to tonight's plans, for having won. . .

If the card games were not the kind of study that was expected
of him, no one complained, and indeed, he had discovered that several of the ex-mercenaries in the employ of Port Security would hold
the start of the evening hands if he was expected. It was a comrade-
ship not quite the equivalent of troop, but then it had become clear
to him over time that he could not expect to find that exact feeling
again in his life.

The feelings he did have in his life now were. . .different. He'd noticed almost at once, starting with looking into a mirror to assure his
readiness for duty after the Captain's order was followed and he'd had
his *vingtai* removed as neatly as mud and blood might be swabbed
off after an engagement. He'd been both surprised and pleased at his
face, finding his aspect not uncomely and his wrinkles not over-set-
ting; he looked younger than Nelirikk Explorer and felt that was,
somehow, an advantage.

More, it seemed to him that it mattered more to him what his
face looked like, and as cut-short as it still was, the arrangement of
his hair made more of a difference to him now. Now, why? Because
now there was not a troop regulation style required of him, nor as far
as he could determine a troop regulation length. It felt odd, but he
was comparing the styles of those around him.

Hazenthull Explorer. . .now that was another thing. If he'd found
his own face acceptable, he'd found hers worrisome, for the anima-
tion was largely gone from it, as nicely shaped as it was. He'd seen her
in the throes of duty, where there was strength and courage and. . .

But there, he was noticing more about the Explorer than her
face, and it had come to him in the night why that might be so, given
the general exuberance he'd enjoyed since his face-cleaning.

The med-tech had apologized for "taking the pair of you into overtime" and that pair, Hazenthull and himself, had been in a unit where rations where short and command stingy in the best of times, and certainly more so after the landing. The only thing they'd not been short of were their inoculations. And in a combat unit those inoculations would have included medical restraints on the distractions of boredom, hunger, and more hormonal issues like anger and sex.

Having divested himself of the outdoors comm unit and running shoes in favor of house boots, he was about to start on his way to his upstairs staff quarters when the security bot rumbled into view.

"Ah, Rifle," the AI said familiarly, in Terran, "I have a message from Nelirikk Explorer that will interest you. He apprises the house that he will be somewhat detained this evening. . ."

Diglon paused, his feet suddenly leaden with concern. It had been a very long time. . .

Turning to face the bot, sorting choices, in his mind, sorting sudden back-up plans. His made plans included a time scheduled ahead with those at Ms. Audrey's, for never before had he had a visit to that place. As he was going as winner of a Poker Night Special at the new Space Port Lounge, there was to be a ceremony as well, as he understood it, a–

"Oh, forgive me, Rifle," said the AI, "please! I had not meant to alarm you! The Explorer informs the House that he has made arrangements for a ride: if you'll be ready at the front door they'll take you directly and on time to Ms. Audrey's, where he'll meet you. He reminds that, in his absence, you should confer with a member of the house about proper dress."

"Can you not suggest proper dress, house?"

There was a pause, which was unusual, and then a nearly diffident reply.

"I have not been long enough in this house, in this place, to feel confident of such suggestions, Rifle, given that they affect many protocols and expectations I do not have direct experience with. I suggest that though I, the cats, and the Tree may wish you well, all of us together would not be able to establish the proper dress mode for a celebratory visit to Ms. Audrey's. Perhaps an adult male member of the household would be best."

Brought to a standstill momentarily, the Rifle stood rooted, gathering to his mind's eye interleaving chains of command, recalling that most things in the house could be sorted out immediately by one resolute person.

"Yes," he said with determination, "an adult male!" Holding his wind jacket close to him, he went in search of the butler in the more formal front of the house, the AI's rumble behind him.

* * *

Alara chel'Voyon Clan Silari, Field Ecologist, Scout, Daughter. . .

Today, she was working in a field far from the Port of Surebleak, and far from her recent haunts of rugged rooftops and near-secret garden rooms filled with old dirt and tired strains of tubers, greens, and vitaplants. She knew her thoughts ought to belong to the leaves she measured and photographed, but Ecologist was not the top role in her thoughts today, *melant'i* be damned.

Her recent arrangements with Conrad, Boss of Surebleak, were as temporary and as nonstandard as any she'd had since she'd been a working Scout: local expenses, food, and housing covered here on this end-of-spiral arm planet in exchange for agronomy expertise and insight. The duties-as-assigned part was not unexpected in a situation where her home-base had been destroyed, the Scout home office couldn't tell her when, if ever, the exploration team she'd been destined for might be reconstituted, and the field situation was elsewise fluid, if not chaotic. Staying *here*, on Surebleak, meant at least some stability in a life and career that was otherwise in extreme disarray. Staying *here* with the tacit connivance of her superiors, was useful. Staying *here* when it was the destination of her soon to be displaced clan. . .was only common sense.

The manual leaf-sorting she was doing was on automatic, which it most assuredly should not be.

Alara, Delm Silari. . .and no, that did not bear thinking on with everything else going on—her delm lived, the clan—if inconvenienced—was intact, and it fell to her to recall her role as Daughter.

All thoughts *must* come back to *daughter*. Her own daughter had gone to Line chel'Mara in a contract marriage before she took on her Scout training, and had been an appropriately squalling and healthy bundle when released into the care of the chel'Mara nurse. It wasn't that child that brought the daughter to mind, but the note that had gone through a tortured line of hold-boxes and Scout tracking to get to her, a note headed URGENT, addressed to Alara chel'Voyon, Daughter of Clan Silari.

In truth, she wasn't much used to thinking of herself in the daughter role, and particularly not in the favored daughter role. It had come to that, though, with Delm Silari, long thought to be bordering his dotage, not unexpectedly favoring the Korval side of the business of the great hole put in Liad by Korval's forces.

Here she sighed, and put the leaves down a moment to wipe unexpected sweat from her brow: sometimes the thinking was an effort, especially the thoughts of these recent events. Korval's retreat into

Plan B, the Scout's suffering a rebellion in their midst, and the attack on Liad itself by the very clan thought by most as the great protector of the planet.

Yes, the attack had been a threat to the home world, but Silari himself had long muttered about the Council of Clans eating up progress for comfort. His having been a deciding vote in allowing the quite young Pat Rin yos'Phelium into Tey Dor's at Daav yos'Phelium's suggestion also figured into the question, but then he'd been a contemporary of that delm's mother.

It should not have mattered, given his age, but he'd promised her he'd not make her delm while she was happy as a Scout, and now things had to change because Silari had been the subordinate business partner in an arrangement generations old. . .and so Clan Forban taking both the other two daughters of Silari–and the daughters of those daughters had not seemed so out of place until the weak-brained Council had thrown Korval off world. Forban supporting the Council, Silari–in the person of Delm Valad chel'Voyon–had opted out of the partnership. Someone needed to be in charge.

Valad was not such a one to be stupid after having made such a momentous decision, and having unretired from the world at large and begun the slow dissolution of business and homestead to vacate Liad along with a hundred other clans, he'd issued orders to the one remaining member of his clan who had not yet fulfilled the second part of her duty to the clan and demanded her duty of her: a replacement heir for herself.

That had been the first shock, but they kept coming, for his orders had included the necessity that she do this soon, without coming home to Liad, in place on Surebleak for the love of space!–because the clan would likely relocate itself there!–and. . .with a husband buy-in price of a pair of cantra now, and the rest to be determined as the clan settled.

Then the surest shock: "The delm wishes this at the earliest moment; my physicians complain of my recent exertions and while I mean to leave them and their strictures both on Liad in the near future it is certain in my mind that we must move forward–that *you* must move forward so that when the clan lifts from Liad your tenure as na'delm may begin in earnest, and with an uncomplicated heir in hand. Changes are happening and it would be good to know Silari will one day be led by a Scout."

Na'delm. Heir to the delm! He was too young to be thinking thus–she was too young. . .

Knowing she was both resourceful and a biologist, he'd leave the choice of an acceptable marriage to her, other than requesting that the genes be of a long lineage, the husband respectful of her and the rules of marriage they'd long followed. And he'd invoked old names and relationships and short list of rules. . .including the hint that if all else failed, she could go to the Delm of Korval, and a reminder that yes, a husband closer to Korval's interests would be closer to Silari's.

So she vaguely sorted leaves, here where plants did better than they ought, as long as. . .as long as. . .as long as something she wasn't sure of happened, and pondered the necessity brought down upon her.

That the Delm of Korval was uniquely available to her, she knew. The delm–at least one of them–was in the house right there, under the tree. As for the other, she knew the Scouts on port included any number willing to bed her. Her doubt was that there were many, given ties of clan and the uncertainties attendant to the evolving role of the Scouts, able to fall in with the kind of wedding-contract her own delm desired, one at least shadowing the proprieties.

Alara found her ankle cramped, and stood, suddenly, letting the leaf stay where it was. She found the work a little more awkward without the Rifle, who often carried, dug, and searched with her. Paradoxically his height allowed him to work closer to the ground it seemed, and he could hold position immaculately in pulling and replacing probes.

He was an odd man, was Diglon, though perhaps not as odd as some of the Scouts she knew, large even by Terran standards and thus huge to her. He'd first been an extra guard to her as she studied the plantings at the spaceport, where he apparently envisioned his role of bodyguard to mean he literally stood between her and threats, daring any such to come through his bulk.

And there was one of the mysteries she'd someday tell her grandchildren about—that she was relying heavily, in the city, on the ability of a genuine Yxtrang to guard her. Liadens were taught to fear and despise the soldier hordes, to consider them forever a threat to the universe, a menace to civilization. And here was Diglon, who a city contact not knowing his background had declared to be a "*pussycat. . .*" of a guard: polite, efficient, watchful, helpful, aware, respectful, honest.

His eye being good and his ability to hand-carry phenomenal, he'd become both guard and assistant during her tour of the in-city grow-rooms and private gardens. He'd been excellent with the grandmothers, especially, who shared as much with him as with her the secrets of their medicinal plots, the special timing of the tuber plantings, the necessity of planting in rotation of these groups, this way.

Thus, she, Liaden and daughter of a Liaden, had swept aside her cultural schooling in favor of her Scout-training, and requested him as her daily guard and then asked he be allowed, later, to accompany her to the fields at Yulie Shaper's place when the farmer himself was unavailable—and then, as the project grew, the assignment became a matter of requesting attendance when his schedule matched hers, and finally, that he be assigned as assistant in title. If he no longer thought himself Yxtrang, then neither would she.

She'd seen him earlier, on his off-day run, but had been unable to acknowledge him, her body shielding an insitu absorption study from the breeze then, and she wondered if she'd missed seeing his return. It was perhaps best, since his concept of duty made it far too easy to hold him over hours, and more than once he'd joined the field work in his own time. It had slipped, at one point, from an exchange she'd overheard between Hazenthull Explorer and the delm's aide Nelirikk, that Diglon's need was occupation.

Standing, the wind buffeted Alara's face, and the smell of soil carried with it grit and a hint of moisture. Her day. . .

Her day, checking the chronometer, had been over sometime before. She laughed, knowing that her thinking had put off thought and action. Her stretch told her the cramp of legs could use true relief, and she began gathering together her supplies. She'd be staying here *under tree* this night, as those of Korval sometimes called it. Maybe tomorrow, before she packed for a five-day at the cramped laboratory in Boss Conrad's block, perhaps tomorrow she could approach one of the house to see if the Korval might spare a moment.

A half-dozen days now, and she'd yet to reply to her own delm. He was not only dear to her, and her father in fact, he was the delm.

Pulling her jacket a little against the wind, she poked a marker into the ground, firmly, so she'd know tomorrow where she had stopped. Picking up her supplies after a final friendly brush at the leaf she'd been studying, she emulated Diglon's march, and headed off. Today, today—right now—she would ask staff to inquire of a moment with the delm.

The protocols of a proper Liaden house in the country might see a member of the clan on door duty assuming a secure situation, else as security an inconspicuously armed doorman or woman, front and back. . .but then Jelaza Kazone, the house, had hardly been a proper Liaden house for these last seven or eight hundred standards and was not likely to start now, nor was a house staffed with a robot. . .

She regretted the robot, at times, as polite as it was. Korval, though, must be seen. . .

Ah, and *why*, Alara asked herself as she approached the door, was she trying to do this by the book now? By the Code itself? With Liad's influence clearly fragmenting, with–

She caught her breath, feeling the urge to back away from her mission strengthening the more she questioned, and knowing that, indeed, she was at risk at disobeying her delm, her father, her....

She *was* a Scout, and knew better.

The rainbow of serenity flashed through her consciousness, and the resolve to do this rebuilt itself before her eyes, as well as the recollection that she gave importance to her universe and not the other way around.

Her delm's decision would not be wasted by her: Liad itself might falter but her clan would hold the loyalty that had supported Korval and the pilots of Korval. This arrangement had kept her clan and her line steady these centuries, and if Liad varied there was no cause for *Silari* to vary.

And so, though she was by rights guesting in the house and able to enter a side door, she still went to the front entrance, and rang.

* * *

Mr. pel'Kana's demeanor so far had been fair, but stern. They stood in the hall; the conversation not loud, nor was it precisely heated. It was pointed however, and Diglon Rifle, permitted presence, was quick to note that the butler and the former butler had resisted going up the ladder of command all the way to The Captain herself, but they had both, without hesitation, referred concisely to the strange bit of Liaden troop lore called The Code as if, in fact, dealing with standing orders.

With Jeeves calling on the necessities of security and the fact that the matter had been referred to him by the Captain's aide, Nelirikk Explorer, Mr. pel'Kana's side of the discussion drew heavily on his own role as butler and head of internal operations for the house, explicitly drawing on the notes of his predecessors as well as the Code.

"I've never had the dressing of a soldier for a visit to a whorehouse, Jeeves. The house is unused to maintaining quite so wide a measure of clothing as you assume; certainly you have access to the records and can understand that the house has not generally outfitted our security–and particularly one of such proportions–for their own private amusements."

They'd both argued around the conflicting bunker of truth that Nelirikk, as the Captain's aide de camp, was able to give instruction to both of them on some topics, as if the order came from the Captain. The difficulty was the bunker pel'Kana had built around his own lack of experience at dressing for such an outing and the necessity–agreed by both parties–that an inappropriate suiting decision would be worse than none at all.

"You have a visitor at the door, sir," said Jeeves in a formal Liaden, which Diglon took to mean both that there was someone coming to the door and that security was building status points against the butler's arguments.

For his part, Mister pel'Kana stood straighter, showing form altogether as nice as that you'd show at a Commander's parade, and waited until the bell actually rang though the hall before moving toward it, and then, pausing to bow and mutter a, "by your leave, Mr. Rifle, I must attend the door," he opened it inward with a flourish.

Diglon, for his part, was surprised—surely the ecologist retained the same privileges he had to enter by the common door near the back staircase rather than the formal door at the front of the house.

Not only did she come by that way, she also performed an extremely elaborate bow, executed to all of them and including the building itself, as she spoke in a Liaden so complex Diglon could only gather the sense of the words rather than know them.

"The house of Korval is of the oldest and most honorable and it is with all humility that I enter. A clan's hope is that Delm Korval will see and advise this one, far from home, with an urgent delmic order upon me and necessity crowding possibility until confusion reigns. As Clan Silari has always acknowledged a debt to the clan of the Pilot, and as Clan Silari follows Korval's lead even now, this traveler seeks a word with the Delm of Korval, that I may be enlightened and empowered to act with propriety in an uncertain moment, on a mission most urgent to my clan. A word, a moment, an audience, I beg of the House, in the name of Silari, with utmost humility."

The butler made a hand gesture that became a lean, that became a bow, his voice firm.

"I hear for the House, oh traveler, and for the House I offer welcome to one on a mission. If you will but accept the hospitality of the House I will ascertain as soon as I may the delm's availability."

The butler bowed her toward a sitting room, but Diglon saw the concern in her eyes and leaned toward her for a moment, catching her eye opening his hands in question. . .

"Please," she told the butler, suddenly bereft of flowery language; "I'll wait here if it isn't long. . ."

pel'Kana bowed to Alara, half-nodded to Diglon before saying, "Your situation is not forgotten," and strode away at a respectful pace, and then around the corner, where his rapid footsteps faded as he mounted the stairs.

"What do you do, my comrade?" Diglon asked her in Terran, "are you in danger? May I aid you?" he bent toward her, voice soft and even concerned.

Alara struggled for a moment with the question, the irony of being named comrade at this moment hard on her sensibility. Her role was stretched across so many *melant'i* points that she could see herself in a play. . .

"Thank you, Diglon," she managed, "Not in danger, but in flux. I'm not sure anyone can help me, which is why I am here. . ."

"If this flux regards the fields, can you share with me. . ."

She waved him off with a Scout sign *allow space, please* and he saw it, hands testing. . .

"Another room?" she heard him venture, and then he admitted, "I have not all of the languages yet, Ecologist, and not all of the forms. There is very much in flux also for me, I fear!"

She sighed up at him, nodding.

"Yes," she agreed, "the whole of the world is in flux, and us within it. But how came you here to be delayed by my needs?"

He moved his hands now, willing to express hand signs if they might work, and she picked up and offered, "A trench across the road?"

He nodded a Surebleak nod of yes, a quick three bounces of the chin.

He raised his eyes to the silent AI, their heights being nearly equal, and spoke distractedly away from her, so she barely heard the edge in his voice.

"I, too, have requested help of the House."

His hands repeated the hole in the road sign, and he continued. . .

"It is not a secret, I believe, that my over-senior, Nelirikk, was to assist me here today, and deliver me to Ms. Audrey's, there to accept my winnings of the card game."

Alara nodded, smiling.

"Yes, I'd heard of that, and it was in the papers that you'd won something. . . congratulations!"

His chin moved again, nodded thanks. "Yes, a win. A double-dip, they call it, and I was much looking forward. . ."

Alara started, suppressing the chuckle while managing to get out. . ."At Ms. Audrey's, this double dip?"

"Indeed, at Ms. Audrey's. I've not been there, and have very little liberty, and now the senior cannot direct my clothing, for I'm told that my work clothes are not appropriate to such celebrations."

Alara nodded in gentle agreement, though aware that Ms. Audrey's front door opened to a wide spectrum of folks. Surely he'd not be turned away if he appeared thus attired.

"I sought assistance," Diglon accused, "of Jeeves, who declares ignorance of the topic. And thus, we have arrived at Mr. pel'Kana's office."

"Mr. pel'Kana," came a sharp voice, "has no experience of dressing for pleasure houses on Surebleak, or anywhere else!"

That gentleman was rushing forward, and gave her a rapid, multifaceted bow, which read out in short as, "By the delm's order, a respectful reply to a supplicant welcome to the House and its comforts."

"I am to inform you, Daughter of Silari, that Lady yos'Phelium is napping with the heir, and that she has left orders to be awakened in time to see you before dinner, which she will do in the ..." here he struggled for a moment, his mouth pursing slightly, obviously quoting verbatim, the Terran falling oddly off his tongue "in the rumpus room, if you don't mind, so the child may wear herself out enough to sleep tonight. If the delm is required for a solving, the delm will be available there."

Alara struggled to regain proper composure, bowing grateful acceptance of the delm's word, daring to breathe. This was a good sign, a delm able to show moderation, a delm. . .

"I shall await Lady yos'Phelium's pleasure, thank you Mister pel'Kana."

He bowed in reply to hers, and Alara thought to go to her room.
. .

She found Diglon's concerned eyes on her, and she gave a wan smile.

"A solving," he asked, "is this good?"

Her breath came easier now, and she gave the half-and-half hand sign, which he knew from their work together. "We only know that when we hear it, my friend."

His turn to nod, and waggle the same sign.

"I wish you success in your endeavors," he said, "And after, if you need assistance, please allow me. . ."

Flattered, she bowed a wordless formal thanks to him while pel'Kana was saying to Jeeves behind him–"You, you have the records of available house clothing–do we even have anything in stores that this man can wear? And how should I know what is proper. . ."

Alara saw Diglon go wooden-faced with worry as Jeeves answered.

"We have many items that will fit Diglon Rifle. I cannot tell you we may outfit him appropriately as a member of Jelaza Kazone's household!"

"Mr. pel'Kana?" she offered.

He didn't hear immediately, having ratcheted up his volume to say, "There are no fashion sources on this planet that I know of, and if you know of them you haven't explained to me how we might. . ."

"Mr. pel'Kana," she insisted, this time moving within reach of his eyes and bowing an eloquent, "offer of information."

"Yes, Daughter of Silari?"

She dismissed that title with the appropriate bow and laughed.

"Oh, no, in this I am a Scout! Scouts are very experienced people, Mr. pel'Kana. I believe, if I may be permitted to assist, that I might be able to discover among your clothes items that, if not appropriate to everyday dress, will be all that is acceptable at a house of pleasure on Surebleak. Scouts, you see, dote on such places; I have seen several sides of such establishments over the course of my studies and I'd be honored if I might be able to assist."

Diglon was nearly radiant, but it was Jeeves who spurred them to action.

"The cab reports itself on the way, Diglon Rifle. You have approximately an hour to prepare."

* * *

"We must use our imagination," she said quietly in his ear, her gentle hands still brushing his hair with the softest brush he'd ever experienced, perhaps lingering on the back of his neck where his hair exceeded troop norm in a style Surebleak recognized as comfortable. She applied a light dressing of some ethereal scent familiar at the edge of consciousness. Alternating with the brush, her hands touched his back, his shoulders, the admonition "Patience, troop, patience. If the fit is not exact, we must make it work, and it must last the evening. Let us be artists. . ."

Surely such attention was reserved for commanders and generals?

Now her hands spanned his back and shoulder, touching skin with knowing hands, for she'd long since explained that the soldier's preferred light sensitive camouflage shirt was inappropriate to such a night. . .though she allowed his chameleonic shorts to be just the thing. . .

"We must be prepared to let inner energy flow, to take full advantage of what comes. . ."

He sighed. His shower over, Diglon stood entranced at parade rest in front of the large mirror as Alara worked, standing on a stool behind him. Mr. pel' Kana, having delivered the last of the "waist clothes" laid across the bed for display, was off now looking for better boots, for neither of the Rifle's two pairs were capable of being "date night fresh" as the ecologist had put it with a wrinkled-nose shrug at them.

"We have no dresser or valets here, Lady," pel'Kana had explained to her, "for the staff situation is not yet stable following our move, and other than Lady Kareen, we have no one at House who might consider such a necessity. And Lady yos'Phelium was quite clear in the matter – 'our Rifle,' she told me, 'is going to a public place, where he is a winner, celebrating an earned victory. It was reported in the news. He represents the House. Surebleak runs on blocks and territories and talk on the street, and he best look *fine* because every local in Audrey's place is going to notice him to start with, and they'll be weighing the house on his turnout and turn-up. He best look *fine*."'

Jeeves appeared after a perfunctory knock on the door, carrying other items, some hung, some not, which he began to display.

On the bed, Diglon knew, there was a kilt-wrap that looked over large, even for him, and of a color that displeased him greatly, as it echoed the colors of the Fourteenth Conquest Corps. Jeeves had admired it, since there was some military history to it which they had not time to explore. He'd held it before him for size and suspected it would be somewhat scratchy if he were careless.

There was a pair of sturdy pants with many pockets – he'd ask after it, later, perhaps, but since he was going visiting he doubted he needed those pockets and suspected he harbored a troop's tendency to regard empty pockets as things to fidget with, or fill. The cloth was sturdy.

The other item he'd not yet touched, and he hoped that when he did that it would fit; it was a pair of slacks, an admirable red-wine color which he'd have never been permitted as infantry. That looked soft and comfortable. It was belted already with a leather belt, it called out luxury to him, and if the Captain wished him to march bravely he'd be pleased to march through Ms. Audrey's doors in them.

"Tops," said Alara, "are important for first impressions. This one, try it on."

She held out a fabric bit that shimmered, white and smooth one moment and then smoother and silvery the next.

As he donned it, she asked Jeeves–"are there other singlets like this, in colors that perhaps match the slacks there?"

There were not though, and it didn't matter. He hesitated, feeling that the sleeveless shirt did not really cover–so much hesitation in fact that Alara smiled at him.

"You have a party, my friend. There's no reason why you should not be as enticing as may be, yourself."

She made a motion he took to mean he should handle the fabric and indeed, it felt good, and too, it did show him to be fit in muscle and tone.

Alara climbed down from the stool and pointed to the antique-styled button-shirt to go over the singlet; it too had shimmer and felt good. So dazzling was it, with a touch of ruff at the collar that he was again afraid that it was no shirt for a simple trooper–but then, he was representing the house, and if the house felt him up to it, so be it, so long as it fit. There was question to that, for surely the sleeves ought to be longer–but Alara soothed.

"Jeeves, surely there is a bracelet or cuff in the house. Matching. Then, the sleeves may be rolled on each arm just so"–here she clinically adjusted them to the length she meant–"and as this is Surebleak, none will doubt that in fact you wish to display your very handsome arms for the delight and edification of others."

Then she patted his arm and smiled up into his face, saying: "You look very well, my friend, and will do the House honor, besides making observers wonder who it is who has won a prize!"

The call came then: the taxi was approaching the drive circle!

Alara stroked three coats that Jeeves held, one in each arm, and Diglon watched her, trusting her judgment in these things now, seeing results already in the mirror–

Her mouth made a silent Oh. . .and then she said it, out loud, "Oh, Diglon, I think this will set you off to look very fine indeed."

He backed away, though, as she held it up to him—a jacket, a leather jacket!

"I must not, comrade, for I surely am not a pilot and none will mistake. . ."

She gave then a peremptory hand motion, identical to the ones she used in field when, from a distance, she meant him to stop a measurement or motion in progress.

"Hush, Diglon," she said to him softly, "we do not ask you to sully honor. Feel this coat—and see the lining? Pilot's jackets are not so lined with simple wool. As pretty as it is, would a pilot trust it to fend off a bad landing? Hardly, but still. . ."

He had touched it, led by her words and her hands, stroking the silky leather. . .

"This is a jacket from the house of Korval, my friend. If it is offered, I would say wear it in health. . ."

She surprised him then by swinging the coat around her own shoulders, where it looked more like an officer's greatcoat than an item of evening wear. . .and she spun, before handing the jacket over, her grin infectious.

"Try it, it must fit because there's no time for another choice! I envy your evening, Diglon!"

It came to him then that perhaps he owed Alara for all this assistance—

"But you can come as well, if I've won a double!"

Mr. pel'Kana's intake of breath was palpable, and Jeeves maintained silence.

Her smile deepened and seemed to take in her whole body, and then her face went blank, and he wondered if he'd overstepped. Surely offering a comrade a visit to a house of pleasure could not be so. . .

She made a hand motion then, of clearing away.

"Dismiss the thought," she managed, almost a sputter; "as much as I appreciate it. Your taxi awaits, there's no time for me to dress properly and indeed, I myself have a pressing engagement on the night. Go, please, cover yourself and the House in glory!"

Rushing his boots, Diglon did as he was told.

* * *

"This way please, Scout," was what Jeeves said, and she followed, wondering if the use of the security bot to call her to her meeting was a subtle warning, a hint, or. . .mere convenience. Her delm had met the bot himself at Trealla Fantrol and spoken of it more than once, the usual result being a discussion of the proper upbringing of a clan's children and the subtlety with which Korval balanced debts...

The room was small and warm, and–soft.

That was Alara's reaction to the rumpus room: soft. Not only were there rugs in multiple depths strewn about, but there were pillows and sit-cushions scattered about on floors and chairs and against shelves, and there were wondrous quilts of multiple sizes draped from chair-backs. There were walkways, cleared here and there, with various plush items that were cats or norbears or dragons or spaceships, and, higher, there were shelves with adult-stuff on them and–Oh!

Barely noticeable on the corner, was a woman altogether Liaden-sized, long red hair wrapped in a spiraling braided coif, who was kneeling, warily watching a child with wide eyes and a wider grin standing, bouncing experimentally on bowed legs, intent and wonder warring on her face as excited but nearly inaudible *whuffs* escaped her smile.

"Lady yos'Phelium," announced Jeeves, "Alara chel'Voyon Clan Silari."

The gray eyes fixed her instantly, smile still strong.

"Please come on in, Scout, over this way," she said—"Pull up a chair, a cushion, a rug—I'm on baby watch tonight."

The eyes had surveyed her, seen that she was dressed respectfully but was ringless, and then gone back to the child, still standing.

Alara was torn by the comfortable informality of the greeting, knowing her mission deserved some seriousness of attention. . .and yet knowing all too well the stricture that one went to Delm Korval only in peril.

And there, she was in peril, for the her own delm felt the clan at risk, and what could she do but. . .

The room was as quiet as it was soft; Jeeves said nothing and the child, after an extra exuberant bounce, settled in front of her mother.

"Good!"

That was Lady yos'Phelium, deftly changing her kneel to a cross-legged seat on the rug next to the youngster, and a hand casually sweeping the closest chair, cushion, and floor in a reaffirmation that they were all the same as far as she was concerned.

Soldier, married to a Scout. Yes, that's what she recalled, daring to go cross-legged herself on the rug, a few hands-breadths away from the child, facing the mother. Soldier-woman, being comfortable in her own house, of a quiet evening, in house boots so light they were almost leather socks. . .not expecting, and perhaps not *wanting*, to deal with bows and layers of protocol.

Already she could imagine herself reporting such a meeting to her father, who'd never think to meet someone in such an informality, but who would no doubt accept that his daughter stood on such footing. . .

"Jeeves, please bring us some morning wine if you please, and some of that spring-cheese we just got from Yulie."

Jeeves assented and started out immediately

"Lady, I must. . ." Alara started, but found herself waved aside nonchalantly.

"How about Miri, while it's just us and Lizzie relaxing, right? As long as I can call you Alara? I grew up hereabouts and some days doing the pretty gets a girl tired. . ."

"Yes, Miri, thank you. . .I am sorry to intrude on your day. . ."

"Not an intrusion; you didn't even have to come through the front door to talk to me, though I have to tell you it did get Mr. pel'Kana's attention. He likes the formal sometimes, and I guess we gotta keep the home folks happy if we can."

Miri laughed, and untangled the baby's foot from the edge of one of the soft rag rugs that populated the corner.

"But anyhow, I need to thank *you*, for helping out with our Diglon. You betcha Nelirikk's going to shine your boots for you one day over this–leaving the poor troop to the last minute over something as important as his first leave on world and then hanging him out for a quick-dress and a cab-ride on his own? And really, not sure I could have done it any better myself, dressing a guy to run to Ms. Audrey's–"

Alara tried to school her face to the idea of a delm dressing a security guard for an evening's romp, but there, Miri had been a soldier, after all, and not just a soldier, but a captain.

Here there was a short break as Jeeves returned with bottle and glasses, and small plates, and a z-gee bulb of something for the baby as well. A tray on short legs went between them and some homemade crackers and a dish of soft-brown cheese.

"That's fine Jeeves; we'll call if we need you."

Lizzie's eyes followed Jeeves' departure with interest; and Miri shook her head over something before returning to her topic, a wry grin on her face.

"As I was saying, I appreciate you picking up the slack there. A good thing, I guess it was, to have a Scout in that mix, else they'd have sent him off in something as ordinary as they could, and that just wouldna done. Saw the vid-feed on his way out to the taxi–you got him right up handsome you did. I seen troops his size couldn't put on comfortable unless it was sloppy. He'll have the city-girls all pleased, I expect."

"Really, it wasn't a difficult thing," Alara said. "He has a sound body to start with, and the choices–well, it works that way, doesn't it, that if you have only a few choices one of them usually looks much better! I merely imagined that I was assisting a cousin with a festival preparation, and the choices became clear!"

Miri nodded, gave the grasping child her z-gee bulb to chase a bit of cracker, and they settled for a moment to sip wine and have cheese themselves. Miri finally deposited an empty glass, and said to her guest in local Terran.

"I was talking about choices afore, and I guess we got some to make here. You already made one, coming to me with a problem, and you say it's a delm thing you got, so you brought it to Korval. How about you explain gentle..." and here Miri made Scout-like hand signs, *simple good quick easy gentle*, "and remember I wasn't born to Liaden, myself, but I can pretty well get by however you want to talk it."

Alara bowed lightly, *simple simple* repeating mildly in her pilot's hands, and laid the basic situation out succinctly, avoiding the formal as much as she could, and also at the end of her explanation, not quite avoiding the spray of water from a thrown water-bulb, the bulb itself snatched out of the air by pilot quick hands.

"Ring the bell and she'll be playing bowli ball if we're not careful!"

Miri handed a small hand-towel to her guest, nodding, and then adjusting the child's position to sit easier against the pillow-back, she sat straighter herself before turning back to Alara.

"Listening for Korval," she said, "I hear that your clan's going through some changes and your delm's dropped you into a hard spot. And I can see what's some behind it, 'cause I hope you don't mind, but I did some research, and pretty much Silari's been one to lean toward Korval almost since that Tree out there took root on Liad."

Abruptly Lizzie rolled from her sitting position and worked her way to standing against the pillow, sharing a self-pleased smile with her onlookers despite a not-quite firm stance.

Miri watched, absorbed for several seconds in the gentle swaying, and then, assured there was some stability there, looked at Alara seriously.

"Don't know we need me to come delm for this, but I can tell you there's a case here, over time, that Silari ought to have a connection with Korval, money in the budget or not. We got council votes, we got old farming agreements, we got help with–heck, Silari Himself knows it."

Alara, startled–it might have been what her delm had thought but the idea hadn't crossed her own mind–raised her hand as if to protest, but Korval was shaking her head gently, hands saying *wait wait*.

Miri paused, pursed her lips, and looked straight at Alara again.

"Just like Silari, though, Koval's a bit thin right now. We got Syl Vor or Quin a few years down the line, but parents are already thinking there, and I'd hate to have to make call for six or eight years out, if you hear me."

Mother instinct, she reached over just in time to steady Lizzie against a sudden rocky step, and turned back, still serious and thoughtful, as much talking to herself as Alara.

"There's Gordon Arbuthnot, but again, he's more out of the yos'Galan side of counting, and not necessarily going to get into the contract stuff. No one's talked about that with me, busy as we all been. Details, all these details."

Now she was touching fingers, and then almost snickered, "I dunno, I think we can't figure Pat Rin's gonna have much free time any year soon," which made them both laugh, even as aghast as Alara was at Korval assuming. . .

"And I think we might need to figure that altogether, we're in a spot with you. I'm doing my part here, but lifemates being lifemates, Val Con's in the same spot as Pat Rin, and if we was to go to bel'Tarda I'm thinking there's another thing would have to be worked out."

bel'Tarda? The rug merchant? Alara ran the connections in her mind, and saw the odd subordinate line–yes, he stood as fosterfather to Pat Rin in the lists, and as old as. . . "Korval," she said, though in reality Korval had yet to be invoked directly in this catalog of potentially available gene donors, "it is my understanding that Silari is not as bold, nor as demanding, nor as acquisitive, as these choices you mention, and which honor me even if not possible. I suspect that my delm, at least, will be pleased to see a contract produce a child of a connection favorable to ourselves *and* to Korval. That our long-connection is fractured I have mentioned, and it is clear that Korval has many more connections within reach than Silari. . ."

Scout-talk in the hands, from Korval: *shredded more nets than we've mended, orbits on remainders still computing.*

Alara signified *read that message and match it.*

The child made a noise that made Alara cringe and Miri laugh. The redhead shook her head, muttering something about being glad when Val Con was back for kid-duty, and then smiled brightly up at her guest.

"So, Alara, I think what we both need to do is to think; and for our side, we'll read the records deep and see if we spot anything to bring to you. Look at the details. If you are thinking of someone else on port, not directly of Korval, it might be good if you could have names and information to hand so that our connections might be considered, and their own needs. Take the day tomorrow to think of it. Certainly I can understand that Silari, moving in support of beliefs, is as worthy as any, and more so than many, when it comes to our consideration. Let us agree that the conversation is not over, and we'll talk in the afternoon, tomorrow. Let us say an hour after the mid-day meal is cleared here."

Taking child to her then, Korval rose, and the interview ended, Alara still in amaze.

* * *

Diglon's night had ended with a quiet cup of whipped-top cocoa, an unexpected gift of the house on his return from Ms. Audrey's in the early hours, brought by Jeeves in his role as night sentry and door master. He doubted that there had been a sleep agent in that draught, yet he'd slept exceptionally well, and was wide awake and well satisfied with himself some moments before the call-tone on the chronometer chirped.

Surebleak, he'd heard from his poker combatants, was a place where the good things were hard to come by, an inhospitable place on the fringe of civilization, a hardship post, a place to escape from if at all possible.

But, in the afterglow of his night, he considered that perhaps not all eyes saw the same world. Here, there was relative quiet, and though the security work he'd been doing was serious enough, there had not been open fighting for some time, and Boss Conrad's dominion was secure, particularly with the backing of the rest of Line yos'Phelium, who could command battleships to stand off planet if need be.

Surebleak–he'd done his research and knew the name of the planet itself to be a sign of the original colonists' disapproval–but there, after their hard work Surebleak had breathable air, drinkable water, and land that could support farms and a spaceport, and–and he'd discovered last night that Ms. Audrey's was but one of a dozen or more pleasure houses! How could port security think it such a burden, when the duty helped make it all safer?

He dressed quietly, taking time to glance out his window into the inner garden where grew the tree and its surround of flowers. In the morning light the usual heavy dawn mist was giving way to dew-topped fronds and flowers, and to the flowers came birds, some few, the winter having been gone some weeks now, and parading about were several cats. Cats amused him, and apparently he, the cats; he was not yet entirely used to them and still, on Hazenthull's standing order, he found he needed lock them out of his quarters else he'd wake to purrs and clothes covered in cat hair.

A motion among the bushes, and from a spot that seemed far too small for him, Jeeves emerged, several more cats in his train. Jeeves offered names to the cats, fed them, communed with them. Truly, Surebleak was a world of marvels, and he pleased to be part of it!

He wondered who else might be seeing the mist drift away. Was the Captain up? That was likely, he supposed, for the baby kept her own hours and he often found the Captain at common table when he arrived, if the one she called Tough Guy were away, as was often the case.

Was Alara the biologist up? No way of knowing that certainty unless he met her: her room was on the opposite side of the Tree's incredible trunk. He'd walked the gardens until he was sure of that, supposing it was his security consciousness at work. It comforted him to know where the folk who were important were.

There was a sigh then, recalling that she was Liaden and her ways were not the ways of the troop, nor of Surebleak, nor of Liad, either, since she was a Scout. She was, however, comfortable to work with and he wondered how he might Balance her assistance for what had truly been a memorable experience. He doubted he should share that he'd thought of her there at Audrey's, for as surely as he would have enjoyed sharing his bounty with her, she'd have cited something from the Code, or from a rulebook, explaining why it couldn't have been so.

A bird, launched by a stalking cat, fluttered very nearly into his window and he knew that the day was upon him, and opened his door, to find two dark cats sitting primly in front of it, as if waiting for him. Indeed, they became his escort, and walked him knowingly to breakfast, their feet avoiding his on the back stairs.

The common table was set; nearby on the old wooden side tables sat the breakfast teas, coffee maker, juices, nut-milks, water, and even the carafe of Yittle, a yeast and caffeine drink he'd asked after one morning and which had been added to the menu. He often started with a few sips of that, and when Haznethull was on station she, too, would have some. He'd been startled to see several other guests partake as he assumed it was a vestige of his trooply upbringing. . .but several claimed to appreciate the robust flavor, and considered it food rather than beverage.

And so, Yittle first, with a side of coffee, and a flash toast of hearty bread brought up from the city. No one else present, he still sat at the end chair, which for the youngsters like Syl Vor or even for the absent Quin and Padi, might be a two-person bench, leaving the places he'd decided were preferred in case others joined. There being rank within rank even here, where so often the unannounced guests might be pilots having left their jackets in the room, or commanders, on holiday, his current spot was the most practical.

A sound behind him as he slathered nut spread on his first flash-toast, and he smiled wide for Alara, who was dressed for—not for field work, but not yet for visiting the city. Perhaps it was her day off.

She'd come in with a commpad and missed his first look; when she did see him she'd already been aiming for one of the seats at the other end of the table, which surely was her right.

Then, seeing no others in the room, the Scout caught his glance and gave a wan nod, changing course to place her keypad across the square angle of the table, to his left side, before angling back to the beverages.

"Diglon, I hope the morning finds you well and in spirits?"

This was said over her shoulder, in Trade.

The words were there, he heard, but her concentration was else-where, he thought, and not simply on the morning duty of her tea.

The languages of this house were slippery. Unlike the small spaceport guard garrison in the city, where the common language was Terran with as much Surebleak dialect as possible, and fell back first to basic Terran, and then to Trade, moving on to Liaden rarely and against custom, to the tongue of the troop not at all, here, sentences might vary language from one to the next, and at times, even with the sentence words, tense, and dialects might be sprinkled about with impunity, and with great accuracy. Even in the presence of the youngsters, who were all now away from house, it was the expectation that communication would take place. He himself was picking up some of this side-language spoken with fingers. Rarely would a sentence be spoken in troop–if the others of his background were there, principally, but then from time from some hidden necessity might come a phrase, a word, even a paragraph or two–not necessarily well-formed–from those two who were Korval, and as well from the elder Scout when he was present.

Yet the Trade Alara offered was a distancing effort, a more formal rather than the everyday. He had recourse to his Yittle, and then nodded, though she might not have seen, agreeing.

"The morning fog found me happily awake; my spirits are high, I am well, and I am rested. And yourself, if I may inquire?"

This, of course, could be shunted aside; their relative ranks being such that permitted casual discussion but did not encourage it.

The musical sound of spoons and ceramics and such came to him, and then she returned, steaming beverage in one hand and a simple buttered cheese roll wrapped in one of the impeccable cloth napkins in the other.

She sighed as she sat, raised her cup toward him as if a salute, and sipped carefully before answering.

"I am well, that I am."

She stopped there, took a bite of her roll, and leaned back into the seat, sipping again soon, stared into her cup reflectively, then tapped on the compad idly to bring forth a screen already waiting. What she might see there he couldn't tell, yet such total distraction was unlike her, and he leaned forward to offer a gentle observation.

"I see you are not dressed for field duty this morning. Have you information or orders for me?"

Her cup to lips, her free hand danced over the keys, and she stared at the screen, sighing, before looking up and bowing a bow of contrition.

"Diglon, you are correct. I have. . .other necessities today, and a meeting this afternoon as well – in fact, thinking of it now, I should have left a message for you that you might also have the day free for yourself. I am behindhand on this."

Now his concern rose, and he weighed his thoughts before making them into words.

"Is it possible that my performance has not been up to standard and that you must make amends with the Captain? I have seen, without understanding, that there has been an issue. I am proud of my posting with you, and your regard, and will do what whatever I may improve. If I may assist your work today, whatever it may be, that we may continue with our studies and bring the fields to full and timely production–"

She startled him, clinking the cup on the table and rising.

She gave him a bow, full of import that he could not read, and then shook her head Terran style, admitting in a quiet voice:

"I have been unkind to you, have I not, these recent days? And you, you with an event of importance I have not honored. We do, very much, need to work as a team and I all foolish to forget. Teammates should help each other."

She paused, spoke a brief line of Liaden:

"Let us do this: give me a moment or two and I shall return and we will begin the morning again, in better Balance. I will put aside this cloud. . ."

She gathered up her commpad, slapping it into clear screen and tucking it into her belt loop, and then quick marched out of the room, placing her used cup on side table and leaving him briefly to wonder if she had pressing physical need. A time passed, of perhaps ten breaths, and she returned.

What exactly she had done in that interim he was unsure; it was said that Scouts had attention exercises and perhaps it was that. Yet she arrived with a hint of energy and awareness that she had lacked on her first entry; and it was if she spotted him for the first time of the day.

"There you are, Diglon," she said now, and a smile touched the corners of her mouth. "I hope your day is well started?"

This was an oddity, but indeed, he had trained well enough to understand when a situation was reviewed and begun again.

"Yes," he managed, and added, "the Yittle is an excellent start and soon I shall move on to meat!"

"And good!"

Now she scooped up a new cup and new tea, and along with that some fruit and another roll. She selected the same seat, and began, as if newly arrived indeed.

"Ah, my friend, I have been remiss; duty calls me to other necessities for much of the day and I'm inclined to permit us both a day away from the field. Indeed, I should have told the House so last night, that you might have slept in after your date in town, for surely a lazy morning would have treated you well!"

She spoke in Terran, with more ease about her.

"I woke easily as I always do," he told her, "and ready to work."

"We shall amend your day in any case, I fear, for the field can use a day or two of growth before we recheck. I'll let Jeeves know you are available, if the House needs you, else, perhaps it would be wise of you to study on what clothes you may need for future civilian use so that we may not have Jeeves and Mr. pel'Kana in such a sweat as last night again."

He laughed despite himself, allowing the image of their rush of the evening before to be the stuff of stories, had he but a troop to share it with.

"Nelirikk Explorer has suggested as much for the future, though I doubt that I shall often win such a prize."

He went silent with consideration of his prize–and after respectful moment she asked him.

"And were you dressed sufficiently finely?"

He nodded, and allowed, "The staff of Ms. Audrey's told me so, and, and in particular Tova was appreciative. The shirts were very fine, she told me, and she took special care to..." here he fumbled, having run out of the correct words in any of the languages he had quick to tongue, "that is, she helped to get me out of them, gently and with much touching, and admired how well they fit, and how well-formed they were for me."

He paused. "I was struck there, with Tova and Diam, that it would have been a good moment for, for. . ." he struggled, started again, "I lack a full troop here, of course, and some events are as good to share as they are to experience. You had paid such attention to finding these correct choices, these choices that helped–and your own adjusting of the clothes had begun to give me the feeling that this was special. I thought that it would have been good if a comrade, a team member, that is. . .had someone like you been there to share in this triumph!"

"Teams," she said, "can do some things together better than others. And some teams, can do everything together. Triumphs. . .some share better than others, I think."

"It would have been good," he said, but honesty took over and he said, "It was good, it just could have been better! And they told me to come back as soon as I might, because I was not so foolish as to be stupid drunk, nor drugged to numb, and I paid attention, which is good and would I please come back. . .they were afraid I was one of the new spacers and would be gone after last night. And for me to dress in fine clothes they thought a present to them!"

Alara laughed, which made him smile, and she said, "Yes, but see, perhaps you can have such a time again and you'll wish to have the dressing of yourself. There's no reason why, in this House, you may not order the clothes you wish!"

"But I am not sure of which clothes there are. I have never seen the like of Tova's. . . undersuit. And then she first and then the pair–they know such techniques as are amazing! I must practice! Did you know that...."

Alara was now eating her fruit, with tea to hand; she was laughing, and in some haste she managed to say, "Perhaps those techniques are discussions for another time and place! Please, do not fail to eat!"

Diglon's stomach agreed with that suggestion, and he rose now to gather his meat and tubers, more Yittle, and some juice. Having thought about the techniques Tova and Diam shared with him, he sighed. He recalled from training that Scouts frequently worked in teams, and wondered how much those teams might share....

Alara sat, brighter than she had the first time into the room, but as she glanced toward the window it was as if a shadow had fallen on her again, or duty pressed, and the edges of her smiled filed off to seriousness.

"Do you know," Diglon said around his food, "That Tova and Diam think that those clothes as you fit me with are such fine things that they are too expensive to have and wear. And Tova wished to

know if I was married, on account of she said she could marry someone in three years, when she retires. . .especially someone who wears
such nice clothes! And I–I am not a commander, I doubt that I can
afford really fine clothes!"

Absently, considering the dressing of him, she said, "You deserve
nice clothes, Diglon, and *here* there is opportunity, because several of
the plants we are looking at make very fine fibers and very fine cloth
as well as food. We can have samples made–you could even perhaps
model them for Tova and Diam as a test!"

Diglon was much taken with that thought, and several others,
and it was only after he realized that Alara had fallen quiet and with-
drawn again that he returned to an earlier topic, and as he spoke he
saw her turn to him, studying his face.

"If it is not my performance that is a difficulty, can you tell me
what I may do to help with this difficulty? It affects how our little
team works. I have been researching the flowers and the food, and
there is so much that we can do–we can grow storage foods that will
have the house eating well all year. . .but the work is important."

He gathered his strength, dropped his voice to nearly a trench-
whisper to insist.

"You must tell me how I can help–I will do extra work, I will do
whatever I may, within the service I am sworn to yos'Phelium. If you
can tell me how to help, you must!"

He realized he'd been leaning toward her, and that she'd been
leaning toward him as well, her brown eyes riveted.

She was silent, and he was, which was awkward, and more so
when they found themselves unalone, the silent Captain standing as
she was a few scant paces away.

"Service to yos'Phelium, is it? Well," she said in Terran, "yos'Phelium's got lots of needs, and me and my other half, we're pretty flexi-

ble. That's why we have folks like dea'Gauss work with us, people who can spin a contract like one never been written and make it look all everyday and acceptable. Heck, that's why we signed a contract to be Road Boss on an outworld."

The Captain's eyes were on him, firm, appraising. Diglon didn't flinch, unsure what the contract talk was about, but sure it was important. She nodded, and said, "You're a good man, Diglon Rifle."

"Thank you, Captain," he said from his seat.

She smiled and added, "You stand with us, right?"

"I do stand with you, of course!"

The Captain turned to Alara.

"He stands with Korval, Daughter of Silari. Just so you know."

"I am informed," Alara said, with a bow, and turned to him–

"Let us walk beneath the tree, Diglon," she said to him, "and you and I will discuss this idea you have, of doing what you may to help. I believe we have many details to discuss!"

ABOUT THE AUTHORS

Maine-based writers **Sharon Lee and Steve Miller** teamed up in the late 1980s to bring the world the story of Kinzel, an inept wizard with a love of cats, a thirst for justice, and a staff of true power. Since then, the husband-and-wife have written dozens of short stories and twenty plus novels, most set in their star-spanning, nationally-best-selling, Liaden Universe®.

Before settling down to the serene and stable life of a science fiction and fantasy writer, Steve was a traveling poet, a rock-band reviewer, reporter, and editor of a string of community newspapers.

Sharon, less adventurous, has been an advertising copywriter, copy editor on night-side news at a small city newspaper, reporter, photographer, and book reviewer.

Both credit their newspaper experiences with teaching them the finer points of collaboration.

Steve and Sharon are jointly the recipients of the **E. E. "Doc" Smith Memorial Award for Imaginative Fiction** (the *Skylark*), one of the oldest awards in science fiction. In addition, their work has won the much-coveted **Prism Award** (*Mouse and Dragon* and *Local Custom*), as well as the **Hal Clement Award for Best Young Adult Science Fiction** (*Balance of Trade*).

Sharon and Steve passionately believe that reading fiction ought to be fun, and that stories are entertainment. Steve and Sharon maintain a web presence at http://korval.com/

NOVELS BY SHARON LEE AND STEVE MILLER

The Liaden Universe®

Fledgling

Saltation

Mouse and Dragon

Ghost Ship

Dragon Ship

Necessity's Child

Trade Secret

Dragon in Exile

Alliance of Equals

The Gathering Edge

Neogenesis

Omnibus Editions

The Dragon Variation

The Agent Gambit

Korval's Game

The Crystal Variation

Story Collections

A Liaden Universe Constellation: Volume 1

A Liaden Universe Constellation: Volume 2

A Liaden Universe Constellation: Volume 3

The Fey Duology

Duainfey

Longeye

Gem ser'Edreth

The Tomorrow Log

by Sharon Lee

Barnburner
Gunshy
Carousel Tides
Carousel Sun
Carousel Seas

THANK YOU

Thank you for your support of our work.

Sharon Lee and Steve Miller